Phonics Focus: vowel + r

THE STORM

BY CHRISTINA EARLEY

ILLUSTRATED BY
BELLA RECH

A Blue Marlin Book

Introduction:

Phonics is the relationship between letters and sounds. It is the foundation for reading words, or decoding. A phonogram is a letter or group of letters that represents a sound. Students who practice phonics and sight words become fluent word readers. Having word fluency allows students to build their comprehension skills and become skilled and confident readers.

Activities:

BEFORE READING

Use your finger to underline the key phonogram in each word in the *Words to Read* list on page 3. Then, read the word. For longer words, look for ways to break the word into smaller parts (double letters, word I know, ending, etc.).

DURING READING

Use sticky notes to annotate for understanding. Write questions, make connections, summarize each page after it is read, or draw an emoji that describes how you felt about different parts.

AFTER READING

Share and discuss your sticky notes with an adult or peer who also read the story.

Key Word/Phonogram: st**or**m

Words to Read:

for	forest	resort
corn	forget	sporting
Ford	fortress	support
form	forty	vortex
gorge	forward	disorder
horn	inform	glorious
north	moral	gorillas
porch	morning	historic
pork	normal	orderly
port	orcas	reporter
shorn	orchard	tornado
storm	ordeal	uniforms
acorn	Orlan	Victoria
airport	perform	
carport	platform	
chorus	popcorn	
Corky	report	

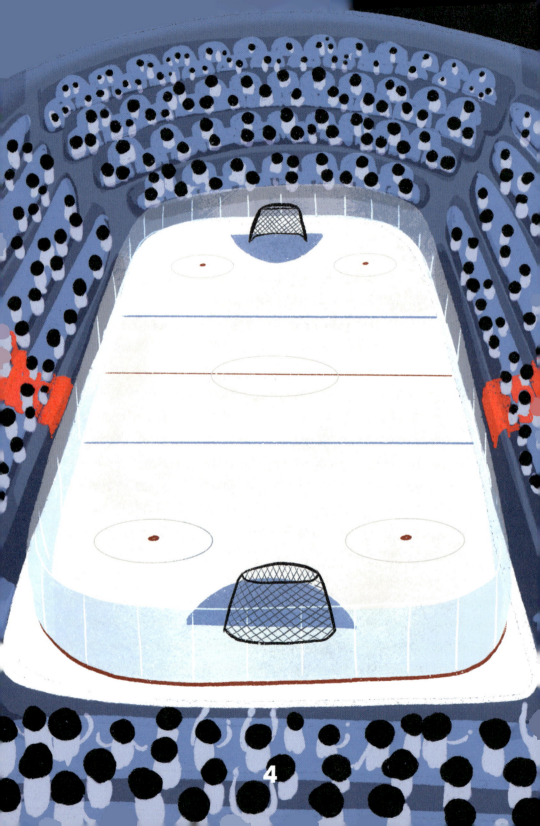

"What a glorious morning for a sporting event at Victoria Ice Arena!" the announcer says. "Today, we have the **North Bay Gorillas** playing the **Ford City Orcas**.

The **Gorillas** are wearing their home uniforms. Get your popcorn for this historic event!"

A horn blares. The announcer shouts, "There's a dangerous storm going through the forest. A vortex has been spotted. It could turn into a tornado!"

Disorder spreads through the arena. Everyone runs to find a safe fortress.

After forty minutes, there is another announcement. "I am pleased to inform you that the storm has passed," the announcer says. "However, it would not be fair or moral to continue the game.

Don't forget to fill out a form for free tickets to another game when things are back to normal. Thank you for being orderly as you move forward."

Fans driving home from the game hear a radio news report.

"I am here at Acorn Resort near the airport," says the reporter. "It looks like a porch and a carport were shorn by the tornado. The vortex went through the orchard and into the gorge."

"The Orlan Chorus will perform at the platform by the port," the reporter continues. "Make a donation to give support.

Chef Corky will give out pork sandwiches and corn on the cob. We must not forget those affected by this ordeal."

Quiz:

1. **True or false?** There was a tornado.
2. **True or false?** The game took place in the afternoon.
3. **True or false?** The resort is near the port.
4. Why was the game stopped?
5. Did the storm cause major damage? How do you know?

Flip the book around for answers!

Answers:
1. True
2. False
3. False
4. Possible answer: There was a bad storm and people had to get to a safe area.
5. Possible answer: Yes, because the chorus is performing to get donations.

Activities:

1. Write an article about how to stay safe during a storm.

2. Write a new story using some or all of the "or" words from this book.

3. Create a vocabulary word map for a word that was new to you. Write the word in the middle of a paper. Surround it with a definition, illustration, sentence, and other words related to the vocabulary word.

4. Make a song to help others learn the sound of "or."

5. Design a game to practice reading and spelling words with "or."

Written by: Christina Earley
Illustrated by: Bella Rech
Design by: Rhea Magaro-Wallace
Editor: Kim Thompson
Educational Consultant: Marie Lemke, M.Ed.
Series Development: James Earley

Library of Congress PCN Data
The Storm (or) / Christina Earley
Blue Marlin Readers
ISBN 979-8-8873-5299-2 (hard cover)
ISBN 979-8-8873-5384-5 (paperback)
ISBN 979-8-8873-5469-9 (EPUB)
ISBN 979-8-8873-5554-2 (eBook)
Library of Congress Control Number: 2022951091

Printed in the United States of America.

Seahorse Publishing Company
seahorsepub.com

Copyright © 2024 **SEAHORSE PUBLISHING COMPANY**

All rights reserved. No part of this publication may be reproduced, stored in a retrieval system or be transmitted in any form or by any means, electronic, mechanical, photocopying, recording, or otherwise, without the prior written permission of Seahorse Publishing Company.

Published in the United States
Seahorse Publishing
PO Box 771325
Coral Springs, FL 33077